# STEVE SHARP

# Meet Steve Sharp

by

**H. L. Dube**

RANSOM

## Steve Sharp

Steve was a cop. Now he works for himself.

2000023171

# BOOK 1

**Meet Steve Sharp**
by H. L. Dube

Illustrated by The Comic Stripper

Published by Ransom Publishing Ltd.
Radley House, 8 St. Cross Road, Winchester, Hampshire
SO23 9HX

www.ransom.co.uk

ISBN    978 184167 390 5
First published in 2013
Copyright © 2013 Ransom Publishing Ltd.

Illustrations copyright © 2013 The Comic Stripper Ltd.

Jaydeen works for Steve.

## Mrs Clayton

Mrs Clayton is rich.

# ONE

Hi!

My name is Sharp. Steve Sharp.

I am a cop.

Why?

I was too hard.

There is no place now for a hard cop.

So I work for myself.

I am my own boss.

# TWO

I have an office.

My name is on the door.

And there is a girl. Jaydeen.

She answers the phone.

15

Yes, I am my own boss.

Nobody gives me a hard time.

And nobody give me work.

We sit in the office, me and
Jaydeen.

Waiting for the phone to ring.

But it never rings.

I am skint.

Jaydeen will have to go.

No money in the bank.

# THREE

So, what is my story?

Let me tell you.

One day this woman comes in to the office.

Says her name is Mrs Clayton.

Mrs Clayton is about 40 years old.

She dresses well.

And she smells good.

Smells of money.

Her kid is missing from home.

Her kid is seventeen years old.

She shows me a photo.

Nice-looking kid.

'Find my girl, Mr Sharp. Please.'

'Sure, Mrs Clayton. No problem.'

We talk about Jo. The missing girl.

Jo Clayton.



We talk about money, too.

Big money.

Mrs Clayton says OK.

Three big ones.

That's three grand.

I want to kiss Mrs Clayton.

I want to kiss the money, too.

Mrs Clayton leaves the office.

# FOUR

'Take this to the bank, Jaydeen,' I
say.

'Be glad to,' Jaydeen says. 'Now I get
some wages.'

I have big money in the bank now.

Three grand is a lot to find a missing kid.

But ... where to find this missing kid?

Seventeen years old.

Before she gets into trouble.

Big trouble.

# STEVE SHARP

Now read
the next
Steve Sharp
book ....